TOMAS LOVES...

by the same author

Can I tell you about Asperger Syndrome?
A guide for friends and family
Foreword by Elizabeth Newson
Illustrated by Jane Telford
Part of the Can I tell you about...? series
ISBN 978 1 84310 206 9
eISBN 978 1 84642 422 9

Can I tell you about Autism?
A guide for friends, family and professionals
Foreword by Glenys Jones
Illustrated by Jane Telford
Part of the Can I tell you about...? series
ISBN 978 1 84905 453 9
eISBN 978 0 85700 829 9

What Did You Say? What Do You Mean?
An Illustrated Guide to Understanding Metaphors
Foreword by Elizabeth Newson
Illustrated by Jane Telford
ISBN 978 1 84310 207 6
Card set ISBN 978 1 84310 924 2
eISBN 978 1 84642 438 0

Adam's Alternative Sports Day
An Asperger Story
ISBN 978 1 84310 300 4
eISBN 978 1 84642 077 1

TOMAS LOVES...

A rhyming book about fun, friendship – and autism

JUDE WELTON
ILLUSTRATED BY JANE TELFORD

Jessica Kingsley *Publishers*
London and Philadelphia

First published in 2015
by Jessica Kingsley Publishers
73 Collier Street
London N1 9BE, UK
and
400 Market Street, Suite 400
Philadelphia, PA 19106, USA

www.jkp.com

Library of Congress Cataloging in Publication Data
A CIP catalog record for this book is available from the Library of Congress

British Library Cataloguing in Publication Data
A CIP catalogue record for this book is available from the British Library

ISBN 978 1 84905 544 4
eISBN 978 0 85700 969 2

Printed and bound in China

To Tomas, Kipper Feet and Flynn

And to the memory of Morgan the Clydesdale horse

Tomas loves watching toy trains on the tracks.

Tomas loves trains that go out and come back.

Tomas loves watching the cars in the street.

Tomas loves books that have words that repeat.

Tomas loves things that have strange sounding names

Like a thingamybob or a flipertyjane.

Thingamybob and flipertyjane

Tomas will say words again and again.

thingamybob

flipertyjane

thingamybob

flipertyjane

thingamybob

flipertyjane

Tomas loves playing with tiny wee toys.

Tomas loves quiet – hates loud, sudden noise.

Tomas loves bouncing on big trampolines.

He squeals and he giggles, he smiles and he beams!

Tomas loves feeding the big heavy horse.

He loves riding as well, being lead round the course.

Tomas loves eating his rice cakes and honey.

He only eats foods that won't hurt his tummy.

Tomas feels safe if he knows what will happen.

If he's stressed or upset, his hands might start flapping.

His mum draws him pictures that plan out each day

And show him when's school and when's food and when's play.

Any change of routine, then his mum has to warn him.

She makes sure he knows what will happen each morning.

His days are planned out from beginning to end.

Each starts and ends with his own special friend.

Tomas loves Flynn – he is friendly and special.

And Flynn loves his Tomas – they cuddle and wrestle.

Tomas loves Flynn, and his Flynn loves him too.

Tomas loves fun and friendship – just like you!

TOMAS LOVES... AND THE AUTISM SPECTRUM

A note from the author

Tomas Loves... was inspired by a young friend of mine who is on the autism spectrum. Rhyming words and Jane's lovely illustrations introduce young readers to the world of autism in an engaging, friendly way. The book aims to help children to see that although a child like Tomas may be different from them in some ways, he is just like them in his need for love, fun and friendship.

It will help if the adult reading with the child knows a little bit about how the things that Tomas loves, and doesn't love, relate to autism.

Children with autism have difficulty making sense of the world: things that happen can seem unpredictable and scary. They feel most comfortable and safe when things are predictable – things such as familiar routines, words that repeat, or toy trains that go back and forth. Visual timetables, like the one that Tomas' mum draws for him each day, help them know what to expect and help to prepare them for changes in routine.

Children with autism often have sensory issues – and may be over- or under-sensitive to things they hear, see, smell, taste or touch. Many, like Tomas, find loud, sudden noises distressing. Some have difficulty digesting gluten and dairy products, and have a special diet. Many children with autism love bouncing on trampolines, which is a fun way to help them to develop coordination and balance.

Although children with autism have problems communicating and interacting with other people, many love being with animals, and have a special bond with them. Having a pet dog to love and care for has helped many children with autism, including Tomas.

For more information about dogs and autism, see http://paws.dogsforthedisabled.org. PAWS (Parents Autism Workshops and Support) is a unique service provided by Dogs for the Disabled.